THE FISHERMAN AND HIS WIFE

WRITTEN BY

THE BROTHERS GRIMM

RETOLD AND ILLUSTRATED BY

RACHEL ISADORA

G. P. PUTNAM'S SONS

In the beginning there was Ada, Ava, Libby, Phyllis and Susan

Thank you

G. P. PUTNAM'S SONS

A division of Penguin Young Readers Group. Published by The Penguin Group.

Penguin Group (USA) Inc., 375 Hudson Street, New York, NY 10014, U.S.A.

Penguin Group (Canada), 90 Eglinton Avenue East, Suite 700, Toronto, Ontario M4P 2Y3, Canada
(a division of Pearson Penguin Canada Inc.).

Penguin Books Ltd, 80 Strand, London WC2R 0RL, England.

Penguin Ireland, 25 St. Stephen's Green, Dublin 2, Ireland (a division of Penguin Books Ltd.).

Penguin Group (Australia), 250 Camberwell Road, Camberwell, Victoria 3124, Australia
(a division of Pearson Australia Group Pty Ltd).

Penguin Books India Pvt Ltd, 11 Community Centre, Panchsheel Park, New Delhi - 110 017, India.

Penguin Group (NZ), 67 Apollo Drive, Rosedale, North Shore 0745, Auckland, New Zealand
(a division of Pearson New Zealand Ltd.).

Penguin Books (South Africa) (Pty) Ltd, 24 Sturdee Avenue, Rosebank, Johannesburg 2196, South Africa.

Penguin Books Ltd, Registered Offices: 80 Strand, London WC2R 0RL, England.

Library of Congress Cataloging-in-Publication Data
Isadora, Rachel. The fisherman and his wife / written by the Brothers Grimm ; retold and illustrated by Rachel Isadora. p. cm.
Summary: The fisherman's greedy wife is never satisfied with the wishes granted her by an enchanted fish. [1. Fairy tales. 2. Folklore—Germany.]
I. Grimm, Jacob, 1785–1863. II. Grimm, Wilhelm, 1786–1859. III. Fisherman and his wife. English. IV. Title.
PZ8.I84Fis 2008 398.2—dc22 [E] 2007018385 ISBN 978-0-399-24771-2
10 9 8 7 6 5 4 3 2 1

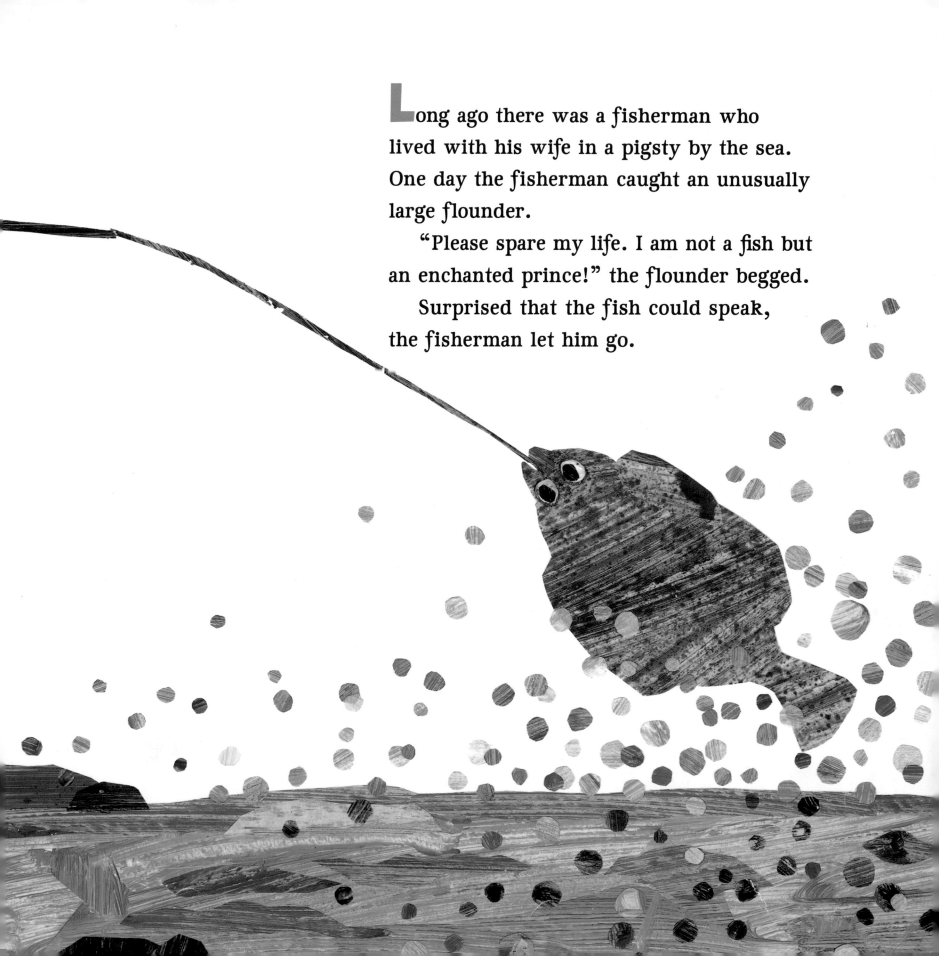

Long ago there was a fisherman who
lived with his wife in a pigsty by the sea.
One day the fisherman caught an unusually
large flounder.

"Please spare my life. I am not a fish but
an enchanted prince!" the flounder begged.

Surprised that the fish could speak,
the fisherman let him go.

When the fisherman arrived home, his wife asked for the fish that she would cook for dinner. The fisherman told her about the flounder.

"Did you not wish for anything before you let him go?" she asked.

"What would I possibly wish for?" the fisherman said. "We live in a place that is small and stinks. Go tell the enchanted flounder I want a hut," the wife insisted.

The sea was stirring when the fisherman
returned.

"Flounder, my wife has a wish," he called out.

"What is it?" the flounder asked as he swam
near the shore.

"A hut," the fisherman answered.

"Go then, she has it already,"
the flounder said.

When the fisherman arrived home, his wife said, "Husband,
isn't this much better?"

"Yes," the fisherman answered, "now we will be happy."

And they were for a few days, until the wife said,
"This hut is still too small. Go, husband, and tell
the flounder I want a stone castle."

The fisherman knew this was not right,
but he did not want to argue, so he went.

The sea was green and murky when
the fisherman called to the flounder that
his wife had another wish.

"What does she want now?"
the flounder asked.

"Alas, she wants a stone castle,"
the fisherman called.

"Go then, she has it already," the flounder said.

When the fisherman arrived home,
his wife asked, "Is this not beautiful?"

"Yes," the fisherman said. "Now let us
be content."

The following morning, the wife decided,
"We should be king of all the land."

"But I don't want to be king,"
the fisherman said.

"Then I will be. Go tell the flounder
I must be king," the wife said.

So the fisherman left with a heavy heart.

The sea was dark and frothy when
the fisherman called to the flounder
that his wife had another wish.

"What does she want now?"
the flounder asked.

"To be king," the fisherman said,
frightened.

"Go home. She is king!"
the flounder said.

The fisherman went home and said, "Now, wife, there is nothing more to wish for."

"I am king and you are nothing but my husband. Go tell the flounder I want to be emperor over all the lands," the wife ordered.

The sea was black and boiled up from deep below.
The fisherman trembled when he called to the flounder.
"What does she want now?" the flounder asked.
"To be emperor," the fisherman called.
"Go, she is emperor!" the flounder called back.

The wife was emperor.
"Are you not satisfied now?"
the fisherman asked.

"No," the wife said. "I am emperor
now but I want to be pope too.
Go immediately and tell the flounder."

The sea roared as it rose higher and higher. The fisherman was very afraid when he called out to the flounder.

"What does she want now?" the flounder asked.

"To be pope," the fisherman answered.

"She is pope," the flounder shouted.

When the fisherman arrived home, he said,
"Wife, you are pope. Now let well enough alone."

But as the sun rose in the morning sky, the wife
said, "I want to be God! Go tell the flounder at once!"

The fisherman was horrified.

"I cannot ask the flounder to do this," he begged.

The wife fell into a rage, and so the fisherman left.

The sea rose with waves as high as mountains when
the fisherman called out.
"What does she want now?" the flounder shouted.
"She wants to be God!" the fisherman cried out.
"Go to her," the flounder called.

When the fisherman
arrived home, there was
the old pigsty and beside
it was his wife!

And that is where the fisherman
and his wife lived from that day on.